For Momma Bear Kelly
and her cub, Axl

BEACH LANE BOOKS · An imprint of Simon & Schuster Children's Publishing Division · 1230 Avenue of the Americas, New York, New York 10020 · Copyright © 2020 by Kimberly Gee · All rights reserved, including the right of reproduction in whole or in part in any form. · BEACH LANE BOOKS is a trademark of Simon & Schuster, Inc. · For information about special discounts for bulk purchases, please contact Simon & Schuster Special Sales at 1-866-506-1949 or business@simonandschuster.com. · The Simon & Schuster Speakers Bureau can bring authors to your live event. For more information or to book an event, contact the Simon & Schuster Speakers Bureau at 1-866-248-3049 or visit our website at www.simonspeakers.com. · Book design by Lauren Rille · The text for this book was set in Supernett. · The illustrations for this book were rendered in black Prismacolor and colored digitally. · Manufactured in China 1119 SCP · First Edition · 10 9 8 7 6 5 4 3 2 1 · Library of Congress Cataloging-in-Publication Data · Names: Gee, Kimberly, author, illustrator. · Title: Glad, glad Bear / Kimberly Gee. · Description: First edition. | New York : Beach Lane Books, [2020] | Summary: Bear is very glad about going to ballet class today, gets somewhat anxious before the music starts, then joyously begins to dance. · Identifiers: LCCN 2019009595 | ISBN 9781534452695 (hardcover : alk. paper) | ISBN 9781534452701 (eBook) · Subjects: | CYAC: Happiness—Fiction. | Ballet dancing—Fiction. | Bears—Fiction. · Classification: LCC PZ7.G2577 Gl 2020 | DDC [E]—dc23 LC record available at https://lccn.loc.gov/2019009595

KIMBERLY GEE

Glad, Glad Bear!

Beach Lane Books
New York London Toronto Sydney New Delhi

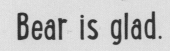

Bear is glad.

He has new leggings.

And new slippers.

And a new tutu!

Today is dance day.

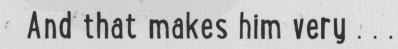

And that makes him very . . .

very . . .

Then Bear is not so sure.

He feels a little shy.

And a little afraid.

And a little different.

But when the music starts,
Bear begins to feel light.

And bubbly.

And twirly.

Then Bear is dancing!

When the music stops,
Bear takes off his slippers
and his tutu.

The teacher says, "Thank you for coming."

And Bear is very glad he did.